Scrappy and Taffy

Lost and Found

Marguerite Turnsey

To order additional copies of this book, contact:
Shrubs Publishing
+61 28006 8158
info@shrubspublishing.com

Scrappy and Taffy - Lost and Found

by
Marguerite Turnley

Scrappy - Lost and Found

Scrappy sat in the old shed at the farm wishing for someone to come and talk to him. Since he'd come to live at the farm he hadn't met anyone who wanted to be his friend. No one would sit and play with him. No one had a kind word to say. The farmer was busy and was always telling Scrappy to stay out of the way. It had been raining all day and Scrappy felt miserable. He couldn't even get warm in the old shed. The wind howled through holes in the walls.

"Get in the truck, dog," said the farmer. "We're going to town."

Scrappy was surprised. He never got to go in the truck.

He felt happy to be moving as he sat in the back on some hessian bags. Wind on his face and the swish of the tires on the road made him feel like singing but the woof that came out of his mouth was more like a croak.

When the farmer got to town he parked in the supermarket car park. He didn't say a word as he went inside the big building and left Scrappy sitting outside the door.

Scrappy sat outside the supermarket shivering. He was cold and wet and he didn't feel well but he stayed there all day, waiting. He watched as people came and went through the big glass doors. He watched as kids came past and patted him. He watched as the same kids came back out of the doors and went away to their cars.

It would have been heaven to go with them and be cared for but he waited for his farmer to come back and get him.

The rain kept falling, the wind kept blowing, but the farmer didn't come back.

It was very cold on the floor outside the big door. It swished open and shut lots of times that day. People who worked in the shop came to the door and looked at him. They pointed and shook their heads as they checked him for identification, realising he had no collar. They went away and came back a while later and talked together. They pointed again and Scrappy felt miserable. A man came out and said, "You can't stay there, dog. Go home."

Scrappy knew he had to stay put just in case the farmer returned for him. And anyway, if he left the door he would only get lost. It was cold and he wanted his farmer to come and get him. He wanted to go back to the farm. He wasn't happy living there but it was home.

Scrappy had lived in the shed all his short life. The farmer was big and rough. He had very big feet, which often kicked Scrappy out of the way or tripped over him. He sometimes forgot to feed Scrappy too, so he had to ask the cats for something to eat. Most of the time they said, "Catch your own mice."

Life was hard for a little dog on the farm but he didn't have anywhere else to go. Then they went to the supermarket and everything changed. Scrappy had been patted many times that day. Lots of kids and big people had talked to him and scratched his head as they went by. But now it was almost dark. His farmer hadn't come out of the shop and he decided to peep around the corner to see if the truck was still there. It wasn't.

Scrappy's heart sank down to his knees. What was happening? Then he noticed another big door and he knew what had happened. His farmer had gone home without him.

What was a little dog going to do? He felt like crying. He did cry. Tears gathered in his big brown eyes and he curled up into a tiny ball on the cold concrete step. He wanted his mother but he didn't know where to find her. He wanted his chooks but they were probably in their pens for the night. They wouldn't miss him until the morning.

The cats wouldn't miss him either. All they wanted was a warm place to sleep and mice. Birds would do as well, but dogs weren't welcome in their circle of friends.

Scrappy wanted his farmer to come back for him but he knew in his heart that he was alone. He had been left at the supermarket because the farmer didn't want him any more.

Scrappy was shivering on the step and wondering if he could sneak inside the big glass doors and find some food. He was very hungry. A soft hand came down and touched him on the head. It stroked and scratched him behind the ears. It felt wonderful. A lady said, "You poor little scrap. You've been here all day."

"Yes," he said. "I've been here waiting for my farmer to take me home."

"I think he's gone home without you," She said. He could hear the smile in her voice and his heart turned over. "I don't think you're got a collar and tag either."

"The farmer didn't bother. He said it cost too much," said Scrappy. Then he started shivering. His tummy growled too.

"Your tummy's growling," said the lady. "I don't know what anyone could be thinking of leaving a poor little guy like you all alone."

"I don't think he remembered I was here," said Scrappy. "He's a farmer and he's busy with chooks and sheep and cows. We live on a big farm a long way away."

"It's getting dark," said the lady. "I think you'd better come home with me. I'll try and find out where you live and get someone to come and get you."

Without another word the lady picked up Scrappy in her arms and put him in her car. She smelled like fresh baked bread and flowers. She had three little kids in the car and they patted him and talked to him. The little girl scratched him under the ears and said, "You're a lovely little doggie. You can sleep in my room."

"No, he can't," said the lady. "He can sleep in the family room."

Scrappy thought they were wonderful. He wished they were his family. He spent the night in a clothesbasket with a blanket. He was still shivering so the basket went in front of the fire and he was given food to eat. He loved it. He said, "This is lovely food. Thank you." Everyone smiled.

The kids went to bed and the lady put Scrappy on her lap and talked to him and brushed his coat until he felt like purring. There was another dog living there and he just sat and watched the visitor. He was called Taffy and was a little terrier like Scrappy. He looked like a happy dog and he grinned at Scrappy. Maybe he wanted someone to play with too, thought Scrappy. He grinned back.

The next day the lady took Scrappy to the vet. The man was kind but Scrappy didn't like being poked and prodded. He didn't like being looked at. He didn't like having the vet give him a needle. He did like it when he was put in the car again and taken back to the lady's house. He was happy to see Taffy who said, "Woof, welcome home."

Scrappy waited all day to be taken back to the farm. He heard the lady talking on the phone and asking if anyone knew him. He was still there a week later when the lady came to him and put him on her lap again. She brushed his fur and scratched his head and told him she couldn't find where he belonged.

She said she was sorry, he had been left at the supermarket and no one had asked about him. Then she said the most wonderful thing. "Don't worry, little Scrap. We'll keep you with us. The kids and I want you to stay. Their daddy does too. Taffy wants you to stay as well. The vet will give you a microchip and a tag but I'll be with you and it won't hurt a bit.

The kid's dad came in and said, "We'll have to get him a collar. We don't want him getting lost again. You're going to have to learn some house rules too, Scrappy. Number one is 'no going to the toilet inside the house'. Number two is 'don't bite the postman'. He doesn't like it. Number three 'is be kind to the cat'. This is her house too. She'll swipe your nose if you aren't nice to her."

Scrappy cried. Tears poured down his furry cheeks and he howled. He was so happy he wanted to sing but his voice came out as a howl. His new kids and their dad seemed to understand. The kids came and picked him up and took him away to their playroom. They laughed and played with him and Taffy came too.

Taffy said, "Well, Scrappy, you fell on your feet."

Scrappy laughed and said, "Isn't that the best place to land."

Taffy said, "Sure is. Want to play chase?"

Scrappy said, "Woof." And the two dogs began to race around the house. They ran so fast the curtains moved. They ran so fast the kids couldn't keep up. They only stopped when mum said, "Okay, that's enough you two. Time for dinner."

They sat down at two bowls of meat and wolfed down the food. Scrappy lay down to sleep in front of the fire in his new basket and sighed. He had found a new home where he was wanted. He had found a new friend in Taffy. And he had a new family. Somehow he knew they would never leave him at the supermarket. He was safe at last. He would never be lonely again.

The end.

A Dogs Dinner

Two little dogs sat under a tree and hid in the grass.

"WOOF! I can see a little rabbit," said Scrappy. "It's playing under that gum tree."

Taffy said, "hey, I can see it too. Woof! Let's chase it."

"No," said Scrappy. "Let's walk over slowly and ask it to come to our house to play."

"Chasing is playing," said Taffy. "We're dogs aren't we? That's what dogs do. They chase rabbits. It's a good game."

Scrappy said, "I don't want to chase rabbits. I like them. I don't want to catch one."

"Why not," asked Taffy.

"Because I don't know what I'd do with a rabbit if I caught one."

"Have you ever chased a rabbit," asked Taffy.

"I have better things to do with my time," said Scrappy.

"Like what?"

"Like guarding the house."

"Do you want to go down to the gate and bark?" asked Taffy.

"No. I want to walk around the fence and sniff."

"Sniff what?" asked Taffy.

"Bad smells."

"What smells bad around here?" Taffy began to sniff the ground.

"You do, Taffy," said Scrappy. "I can't remember the last time you let the kids bath you. You really need some shampoo and a brush. Then I might let you be a guard dog with me."

"I don't smell that bad," said Taffy. "You smell worse."

"Of course I do," said Scrappy. "I need to smell horrible so no-one will try to come into the house. They will sniff me and leave. I'm the guard dog."

"What if they are nice visitors?"

"Then I'll tell them to come in and they won't care that I smell bad."

"I'm not sure that will work, Scrappy."

"Why not, Taffy?"

"Because if you smell bad, we won't be able to sniff out the real bad visitors. They'll be able to sneak into the house and take away things."

"Like what?" scoffed Scrappy.

"Like our beds and our dinner bowls."

"Who would want our bowls.? They'll be empty."

"No they won't. It's dinner time and Mum has just put

food in them."

"Why didn't you tell me before you silly terrier."

"You didn't ask," said Taffy. "You're always telling me to keep quiet so I did."

"I didn't mean to keep quiet when Mum has food for us. You're supposed to tell me and then we can go and eat it."

"Oh. Well, there's food there Scrappy."

"Great. My tummy is so empty I could eat plastic."

"Woof, Woof. Come quick Scrappy. I just looked in the kitchen. There was food in your bowl but Sammy the cat ate it."

Scrappy barked very loud. "What?"

"There's no need to yell at me Scrappy. I didn't eat your tea."

"No," said Scrappy. "But I'm going to eat yours."

Taffy and Scrappy ran through the house. They ran around and around until they skidded on a rug and fell in a heap. When they reached their food bowls they found Sammy the cat licking his paws and cleaning his face.

"Meow. Thanks for the dinners guys," Sammy said. "They were delicious."

"You ate both our dinners," growled Scrappy.

"You shouldn't have done that," said Taffy.

Sammy grinned and said, "I know." Then he began to run. He ran through the house. He jumped up on beds. He climbed up curtains. He laughed and yowled like a wild cat but Scrappy and Taffy couldn't catch him.

Sammy ran out into the back yard. He raced up a tree then sat up on a branch looking at Scrappy and Taffy who were barking and trying to climb up too. He laughed.

"Woof," said Scrappy. "I'm going to wait all day, Sammy."

"Woof, woof," said Taffy. "I'm going to wait all night."

"Don't bother to wait," said Sammy. He laughed again. "I can jump from tree to tree in our yard and you won't ever be able to catch me. I'm too clever."

"You're a naughty cat," said Scrappy.

"We're going to wait a long time," said Taffy. He yawned. "All night long."

Then Taffy lay down and went to sleep. He was tired after all that running and chasing. He was so sleepy.

Scrappy sat and watched. He wasn't going to sleep. He knew Sammy would have to come down sooner or later. And when he did, Scrappy would be waiting.

Scrappy was still at the foot of the tree when Sammy came down. He was snoring. Taffy was snoring too. Sammy tried not to laugh. He knew how to escape.

He went inside the house through the cat door. He ran through the house quietly, tiptoeing so he wouldn't wake any people up. Then he hid inside the linen cupboard.

When Scrappy and Taffy woke up, they knew Sammy had gone. "Where is he Scrappy?" asked Taffy. "He isn't in the tree."

"No," agreed Scrappy. "He's nowhere in the yard. Let's look inside the house. He can't be far away."

They looked everywhere but the cat had disappeared.

Sammy sat inside the cupboard and grinned. He said to himself, "I can stay here all day. And when those silly dogs get fed again, I'll be there to clean their bowls for them. I'm going to enjoy that."

"Don't get too pleased with yourself," said Scrappy from outside the cupboard. "We know you're in there Sammy. We heard you talking to yourself."

"Meow," yowled Sammy. "I'm a poor little cat. I'm locked in."

"Woof," said Taffy. "Let him out Scrappy. He's a poor little cat. He sounds hungry."

"He's pulling your leg Taffy," said Scrappy. "We don't believe you Sammy."

"Whatareyougoingtodo," askedSammy. Hesharpened his claws on the carpet and got ready to run.

"Mum has just put your dinner on a plate. We've eaten ours so we want you to clean our dishes while we eat your tea as well. It's only fair."

"Meow. That's not nice. How am I going to wash dishes?" asked Sammy.

"You can stand on a chair and put the dishes in the sink," said Taffy.

"But I'm a cat," said Sammy. "I can't wash dishes."

"You can learn," said Scrappy. "We did."

"Yes," said Taffy. "And you can dry them too."

Sammy groaned. He would rather catch mice than wash and dry dishes.

When Scrappy had filled the sink with water, Taffy tipped some detergent in. Sammy came out of his cupboard and climbed up on the chair. He knew the dogs wouldn't let him escape without doing his duty.

He washed the two bowls and was about to let the water out when he slipped and fell into the water. He got wet all over. He began to yowl. He sniffed and howled and shook himself all over the two dogs.

They barked and barked. "This is a good game," said Taffy.

"This is a silly game," said Scrappy.

"This is not a game," said Sammy.

Sammy crawled down off the chair and shook himself. He sat in front of the heater and tried to clean himself with his tongue. He was so wet the floor rug got wet too. He sniffed and he yowled as he tried to get dry.

Scrappy took pity on him. "Here Sammy," said Scrappy. "I'll turn the heater up to high." Sammy shook himself so that water flew everywhere.

"I'll find you a towel," said Taffy. He ran to the bathroom.

The dogs were as wet as Sammy so they all sat in front of the heater to dry. They all rubbed their fur with the towel and sneezed because they were wet and cold.

Then, because they were all tired out, they lay down and fell asleep. They snuggled up together in a pile of arms and legs and feet. They kept each other warm and cozy all night long. Taffy dreamed of tiny rabbits. Sammy dreamed of giant mice. Scrappy dreamed of catching fish. They all snored the whole night long and you couldn't tell them apart.

The End